The Winchester Mysteries

The Missing Necklace

Alexis Schmitz

Disclaimer: This book is a work of fiction. While inspired by historical people, locations, and events, significant elements, characters, and details have been fictionalized for dramatic purposes. Names, characters, places, and incidents are products of the author's imagination or are used fictitiously. Any resemblance to actual events or persons, living or dead, is entirely coincidental.

ACTIVITIES & EXPLORATIONS

For learning activities and explorations to accompany "The Winchester Mysteries: The Missing Necklace," visit the series website at WinchesterMysteries.com.

DEDICATION

For my children, Ashur, Aidin, Elyas, & Ayla; thank you for being my constant reminders of the value of creativity, hard work, curiosity, and determination.

Contents

Acknowledgements

I'm incredibly grateful to The Winchester Mystery House for their dedication to preserving this captivating historic site. Their commitment has allowed me to craft a story that pays tribute to its enigmatic past. Thank you also to History, San Jose for their extensive collection of historical photographs, which add depth to the narrative. Special thanks go to my mom, Glenda, for her invaluable editing, and to Chris for his support. To all the readers, especially young ones, who have been captivated by the Winchester House, thank you, and I hope you enjoy this book.

The Winchester Photo Album

The Winchester House

Courtesy of History, San Jose

Carl and Theodore Hansen

Courtesy of History, San Jose

Mrs. Winchester's dog, Zip

Courtesy of History, San Jose

A woman in an automobile at the Winchester House

Courtesy of History, San Jose

1 Growing Curiosity

The warm sun rose in the clear blue sky, the air carried the sweet scent of the flowers blooming on the rows of fruit trees which created a patchwork of orchards. Apricots, plums, and cherries were the primary crops in San Jose, California in the early 1900s, but something else was growing amidst the orchards - Lily Rivera. Lily's long brown hair fell past her shoulders, her hazel eyes were ever alert for adventure and exploration. Lily had been raised among the fruit trees, basking in the warm California sunshine, just as her family had for generations. A few farms away, another remarkable growth was taking place — the Winchester House.

Initially, the Winchester House had been like many other farmhouses in the area. It was comfortable and sturdy, with a porch that overlooked the surrounding orchard. However, everything changed when Mrs. Sarah Winchester, one of the wealthiest women in the country, arrived in San Jose and purchased the eight-room farmhouse. From that point on, the house started growing, much like Lily, among the fruit trees and under the California sun. Rooms were added on and then torn down, towers rose and were then enfolded by newer additions.

The farmhouse Mrs. Winchester bought in 1886 had vanished, obscured by a labyrinth of intricate rooms, elaborate porches, and colorful stained glass windows. It was now covered by delicate spires and towering structures that soared into the sky. The grandest tower, rising five stories high, surveyed the orchards and the scattered trees that grew across the wide front lawn. The mansion boasted beautiful woodwork, from the intricate trim of the arched windows, to the numerous detailed inlays on the walls, from the delicate carved columns of the porches, to the lattice work of the roof walks. There was so very much to see on the outside of the Winchester House which only led to more curiosity about the woman who made the house her home.

Mrs. Winchester was a highly respected and highly private woman. Her mysterious presence and limited public knowledge about her led the local community to wonder about what she might be doing at the amazing house. While most people were content with their own imaginative tales and gossip, Lily was different. She possessed a curiosity that couldn't be satisfied with mere speculation. She craved the truth. And so, one summer day, her curiosity led her through the orchards towards the Winchester House.

A little over a decade had passed since Mrs. Winchester had purchased the house. Construction had been ongoing ever since. Lily had heard countless rumors about the house she grew up alongside. Some people said that Mrs. Winchester kept the building going, day and night, because the sounds of construction kept away the ghosts she feared. Others said Mrs. Winchester kept building because she was trying to build a connection to the spirit world, where her dearly departed husband and daughter were. Lily had listened to all the rumors with interest, and this summer, she decided to let her curiosity guide her. And she knew exactly who could help her in her quest for answers.

The large work yard behind the Winchester House buzzed with all types of busyness. The whir of machinery as timber was smoothed into newly cut boards. The rhythmic clinks and metallic whispers as metal pipes of all lengths and shapes were arranged and connected for use bringing water right into Mrs. Winchester's home. And there was the seasonal work of summer, harvesting the fruit trees and packing crates of fruit to be taken to the processing sheds or the market. The Winchester House's backyard differed from any other farmhouse Lily had ever seen. It was filled with workshops, tool sheds, and storage barns of all kinds. Men moved around with unfamiliar tools, pipes, and wires. It was easy for a slim, brown-haired girl dressed in a simple pinafore to watch the commotion unnoticed from the sidelines.

As Lily stood there observing, she saw the boys she was searching for. They were easy to spot — running, laughing, and shouting through the bustling yard. The older boy, with tousled light brown hair and a determined expression, led the way, holding what appeared to be a tin toy car, while the younger one, blonde with smudges of dirt streaking his cheeks and leaves in his hair, followed, making a ruckus. Lily waited until they drew near before revealing herself.

"Hey there," Lily cheerfully greeted, reaching out her hand.

The older boy's laughter came to a sudden halt, and the younger boy, about seven years old, quickly snatched the toy car with one hand while shaking Lily's outstretched hand with the other. "Well, hello to you too," he replied, flashing a grin with several missing teeth.

The older boy recovered from his surprise, wiping his brow on his forearm. "Aren't you that girl from school?" he asked. The boy stood almost as tall as Lily and was dressed in worn denim overalls and sported canvas sneakers.

"Yes, that's me, I'm Lily Rivera. I live nearby, just over that way," Lily explained, pointing over her shoulder.

"I'm Carl, and this is Theodore, my brother," nine-year-old Carl said, gesturing towards his grinning sibling clutching the toy car. Theodore was clearly wearing the same overalls and sneakers, only several sizes smaller, most likely the very ones Carl had worn during summers past.

2 Helping Hands

Standing beside Carl and Theodore, Lily glanced around the bustling work yard, observing the flurry of activity that unfolded before her eyes. Men hurried about, carrying wooden boards from the nearby sawmill, while others carried buckets and trowels, ready for a building project. Other workers hunched over large sheets of paper, carefully jotting down notes and measurements.

"There sure is a lot happening here today," Lily remarked, her voice filled with interest, as she took in the scene.

"There's always something going on around here," Theodore proudly declared, surveying the busy work yard.

Carl and Theodore's father, Mr. Hansen, served as the foreman of Winchester Ranch, and was entrusted with overseeing all the construction projects on the ever-growing Winchester House. That meant the boys were usually well-informed of the latest news regarding the ongoing work and upcoming projects. Every morning, Mrs. Winchester met with their father to discuss progress and share her new ideas. Mr. Hansen would then emerge from their discussions and oversee the work crew, directing carpenters, masons, and other skilled laborers. Carl and Theodore, keen to learn every detail, often trailed alongside their father, eagerly listening to the latest developments.

As the trio strolled through the lively work yard this summer day, Lily caught sight of a large wooden crate. Its lid was removed, resting to the side, revealing a remarkable sight. Inside the crate, heaps of gray and cream colored wool were piled up. The wool looked clean and combed, with all the wool hairs arranged in the same direction. Curiosity brimming, she approached the crate which reached her waist.

"What's all this wool for?" Lily wondered, her gaze fixed on the soft, fluffy material, "Is someone about to knit a hundred sweaters or something?" Her words elicited laughter from the boys, and Carl stepped forward to provide an explanation.

"This wool is for the walls of the house," Carl revealed, scooping up a handful of the plush, gray fibers. "Mrs. Winchester wants this wool put into the walls of the house while they get built."

Lily's eyes widened in amazement. "Wool in the walls of the house? Why would anyone want to do that?" She fanned herself with her hand to emphasize the heat and exclaimed, "It's hot enough as it is!"

"You might think that the wool would make the house hotter," began Carl, "but it actually helps keep it cooler..."

"And warmer," Theodore added, eager to contribute, "It keeps the house cooler during the summer and warmer in the winter."

Lily raised an eyebrow doubtfully, so Carl continued, "You see, the wool acts as a barrier. It keeps whatever is happening outside, outside. So, if it's hot outside, the wool helps keep the heat out. And if it's cold outside, it helps keep the cold out."

Lily's eyes widened in surprise, a spark of newfound understanding showing on her face. "That's truly amazing," she declared, her gaze once again drawn to the impressive pile of wool before her.

At that moment, a lanky teenage boy with dark hair appeared, pulling an oversized handcart alongside the crate. Frank was a local boy who worked with the Winchester crew in the summer. Theodore's face lit up with recognition as he greeted the newcomer.

"Hey there, Frank," Theodore exclaimed, a wide grin stretching across his face.

Returning the smile, Frank reached out and playfully tousled Theodore's blonde hair. "Hey there yourself, Theodore," he replied fondly. He then turned to Carl, nodding warmly. "Hello, Carl." Then his gaze landed on Lily.

"And who might this be?" asked Frank, his voice filled with interest.

"This here is Lily," said Theodore, gesturing at Lily with his thumb.

With a shy smile, Lily introduced herself. "Hi," she said softly.

"Nice to meet you, Lily," said Frank amiably, "don't let these two rascals get you into too much trouble around here," he grinned with a playful twinkle in his eye.

Theodore burst into laughter, while Carl shook his head in mock disapproval. Then Carl gestured at the handcart and asked, "So, what are you up to, Frank?"

"Well," Frank explained, "we're working on the walls on the new section of the west side of the house. It's time to add the wool insulation, so I'm here to gather some of this wool and cart it over to the construction site."

Excitement radiated from Theodore as he joined Frank at the cart. "We'll help you, Frank," he offered, positioning himself beside the handcart.

"Absolutely," Carl chimed in. "We'll have that cart loaded in no time."

"Alright then," said Frank, putting his hands on his hips. "They say two pairs of hands makes light work, so with four pairs of hands, this will feel like hardly any work at all."

Without further delay, the children and Frank began grabbing armfuls of the prepared wool from the crate and loading it into the cart. The wool was light and occasionally loose bits were snatched by the breeze, making the children laugh as they chased the fluffy wisps across the work yard.

Once the handcart was brimming with wool, Frank thanked the children for their help and set off towards the construction site. Meanwhile Lily, Carl, and Theodore made their way to the nearby water pump, where a few tin cups awaited anyone thirsty from their labors. Carl diligently pumped the handle, and Theodore caught the water that gushed out in three cups, passing one to Lily, one to Carl, and finally taking a long sip from his own cup. The water was refreshingly cold and delicious.

From that early summer day forward, Lily began waking with the sun, completing her chores swiftly, and making her way to the Winchester Ranch. Upon her arrival, the boys eagerly greeted her, ready to share exciting tidbits about the plans they had overheard or proudly show her pieces of the materials that would be used in constructing the house.

3 Discovery in the Barn

On a bright morning in the middle of June, Lily arrived at the Winchester work yard to find Carl and Theodore eagerly waiting for her.

"Lily!" exclaimed Theodore, unable to contain his excitement. "We have to show you something!" He turned and darted towards the barn, beckoning Lily and Carl to follow.

Curiosity raised, Lily hurried after Theodore while Carl followed with a knowing smile. They entered the well-built barn, its sturdy beams arranged in even rows. The scent of fresh hay filled the air and sunlight streamed through the open barn doors, casting a warm glow. Bales of hay, stacked neatly against a wall, created cozy nooks which had become temporary homes for a few fortunate birds. Well-honed pitchforks and shovels with sharp edges and polished wooden handles hung next to well-oiled harnesses, which were smooth and bright, ready to be used for harnessing the farm horses. And in a large pen, overlooking the nearby orchard, stood a magnificent light brown cow.

Theodore approached the pen with a calm manner. "Isn't she beautiful? And feel her, she's so soft." He extended his hand, and the cow turned her head, and gently pressed her velvety cheek against his palm.

Carl and Lily joined Theodore beside the pen. "She arrived yesterday evening," Carl explained. "Miss Daisy told us that if we stay calm and speak softly around her, she'll grow accustomed to us in no time."

"The cow told you that?" Lily asked, perplexed.

Carl and Theodore burst into laughter, quickly muffling their amusement to avoid startling the cow. "No, no," Theodore managed to say amidst the giggles. "The cow's name is Lulubelle. Miss Daisy is Miss Daisy."

"Miss Daisy has a deep love for all kinds of animals and wants to ensure that Lulubelle settles in comfortably," added Carl."

Lily smiled at her own mistake and leaned over to pat Lulubelle's side. "My apologies for the confusion, Lulubelle. I'm delighted to meet you."

The trio continued doting on Lulubelle until Theodore decided to find a carrot to offer her.

When he returned to the barn, Theodore held a carrot in one hand and was pulling a smiling young woman along with the other. "Look, Lily, I found Miss Daisy! Now you won't mistake her for a cow!" Theodore laughed.

Lily blushed and nervously fidgeted with her hands. She had rarely encountered such an elegantly dressed lady before. Miss Daisy radiated charm, her dark hair nestled beneath a tilted blue hat. Dressed in a fitted blue skirt with a slight flare which reached her ankles and a well-fitted jacket with shiny buttons and a large polka dot bow at the collar, she was clearly a woman of modern style. Then, Lily glanced down at her own worn, dusty shoes and her short dress, with its hem let out as much as it could be, inching perilously close to her knees.

"Now, Theodore," Daisy said, laughing, "please give me a proper introduction to your friend."

"Sorry, Miss Daisy," Theodore apologized. "Lily, this here is Miss Daisy, and Miss Daisy, this here is Lily. Lily goes to our school, but now she's our friend too."

Lily blushed once more. "It's a pleasure to meet you, Lily," Daisy said, clasping Lily's hand and looking her in the eyes with a warm smile. "And I see you've already met our newest addition." Daisy stepped forward, giving Lulubelle's side two firm pats. "She's truly a remarkable beauty, don't you think?"

"Yes, ma'am," Lily replied softly. But then, she remembered her determination to follow her curiosity wherever it led her and spoke more surely. "I live on a nearby farm, ma'am. We don't have any cows, but we do have some lovely chickens and two plump, pink pigs named Nan and Patches."

"Nan and Patches," Daisy repeated. "They sound delightful. Perhaps someday I'll have the chance to meet them."

Theodore cupped his hand around his mouth, leaning towards Lily, and whispered loudly, "See, I told you she's crazy about animals."

"Theodore!" Carl chided, playfully swatting his brother's arm. Theodore simply shrugged.

"That's alright, Carl. Theodore is correct," Daisy said, smiling. "But now I must go see Aunt Sallie. You all enjoy yourselves." With a final pat for Lulubelle, Daisy gracefully exited the barn.

The children watched Daisy as she headed toward the enormous Winchester House.

"Does Miss Daisy's Aunt Sallie work in the house?" asked Lily wonderingly, her eyes passing over the ever-expanding floors, windows, and towers of the yellow house.

The boys looked at Lily and then at each other in surprise. "Miss Daisy's Aunt Sallie is Mrs. Winchester," explained Theodore.

"Mrs. Winchester!" exclaimed Lily.

"Yep," said Carl knowingly, "the one and only - richest lady in California and owner of this whole house and ranch."

4 An Unexpected Invitation

When Lily arrived at the Winchester House on her next visit, she immediately noticed a sense of excitement in the work yard. There was a large delivery wagon in the driveway which in and of itself wasn't that odd. Although the workshops on the property supplied a great deal of what went into the house, Mrs. Winchester also often ordered specialty goods from San Francisco and other far-off places. Colorful paints, fancy carpeting, and decorative tiles would arrive from afar to be added to the beauty of the Winchester House. Miss Daisy, standing by the side of the wagon, called out to Lily and waved her over.

"Lily, you simply must see this!" Daisy exclaimed. Lily hurried to Daisy's side, where a man carefully unrolled a section of beautifully patterned paper that shimmered gold in the sunlight. It had a captivating sparkle unlike anything Lily had seen before. She instinctively reached out to touch it, but the man pulled it back slightly.

"It's perfectly fine, Mr. Dawes. Once it's on the walls, it will, no doubt, entice many people with its beauty," Daisy reassured him, gesturing for Lily to come closer.

Lily gently traced her finger over the surface of the shining paper and asked the man, "Why does it sparkle like that?"

"It has a special stone in it," he replied. "This is the first time I've delivered so many rolls of this paper. It came all the way from France." Mr. Dawes rolled the paper back up and went to the rear of the wagon.

Daisy's eyes shifted towards Lily with a glint of appreciation. "Lily, it's my good luck that you arrived when you did," she remarked, her excitement still palpable from the arrival of the exquisite wallpaper. "I have a few packages in my motor car, more than I can handle on my own. Would you be a dear and lend me a hand in taking them upstairs?" Miss Daisy asked leading Lily away from the wagon and over to her motor car.

When Miss Daisy's black motor car had been delivered to the Winchester Ranch, its striking presence was the talk of the town. The townsfolk, captivated by this remarkable innovation, eagerly gathered to catch a glimpse of the amazing machine. With its strong metal frame and polished wooden panels, the motor car stood proudly on four spoked wheels, each fitted with rubber tires that hugged the dusty roads. Most folks had never seen a motor car, and while many were excited to see yet another amazing innovation brought to the valley by the Winchester Ranch, some were upset speculating that the motor car was dangerous and would surely cause accidents.

Lily's heart raced with excitement. "Of course! I'd be happy to help," she replied, eagerly following Miss Daisy to her shiny black car. Daisy handed Lily a hat box and several wrapped packages, then picked up the remaining parcels and closed the car door.

While Lilly had been delighted with her days spent with Theodore and Carl in the Winchester work yard, she had never stopped hoping for a chance to go inside the magnificent house, and now that chance had arrived. Following close behind Miss Daisy, Lily passed through the small back garden where delicate flowers bloomed, their petals swaying gently in the breeze. Lush greenery framed the garden and, in the center, an enchanting gazebo stood, its frame covered with vines and climbing roses. Sunlight filtered through the lattice walls, casting dappled patterns on the cobblestone pathway. The air was full of the sweet fragrance of blossoms. Daisy paused at the back door to shift the packages and turn the doorknob, and then they were inside.

The hallway stretched out before Lily, the lower half of the wall was honey-colored wood carved with a pattern of inset squares, the upper half a wallpaper adorned with striking ruby-red flowers set amidst delicate winding vines. The glossy wood floor mirrored the sunlight streaming in from windows set high on the opposite wall. Although her arms were filled with Miss Daisy's packages, Lily couldn't help but shift them to free a finger to run along the carved designs, marveling at the smooth woodwork.

Lily followed Daisy deeper into the house, their footsteps echoing in the vastness of the rooms. The ceilings soared high above, with grand chandeliers that sparkled and twinkled like stars. Sunlight poured through stained glass windows, casting bright colors on the walls and floors.

Each room held its own secrets and surprises. In one room they passed, Lily glimpsed an enormous fireplace, its hearth big enough for her to stand in. Surrounding the fireplace, towering shelves stood proudly, displaying a collection of mysterious treasures - a beautifully made crystal vase with delicate patterning, an ornate porcelain figurine capturing a moment in time, and a feathered mask, its bright colors and striking design hinting at distant lands.

Up they climbed, the curving stairs guiding them towards Daisy's charming room. When they arrived, Lily saw that the walls of Daisy's room featured wallpaper depicting a bright and cheerful daisy pattern. Sunlight cascaded through an open window bathing the room in a warm glow. Near the window with its view of the fields of the valley, a cozy chair beckoned with plump cushions and a stack of books on the table beside. On the opposite wall, stood a dressing table, its surface decorated with colorful cut glass bottles and sparkling jewelry. The large four-post bed took center stage in the room. Its wooden posts rose tall, carved with delicate flowers and draped in sheer fabric that whispered with every passing breeze. Layers of plush pillows and lush linens offered a promise of immense comfort. Next to the bed, a bedside table held cherished photographs. The room itself was a haven of peacefulness.

Lily's attention was pulled from the charming room as Daisy exclaimed gratefully, "Lily, you're a lifesaver! Could you please set those packages down on the bed for me?"

Lily nodded, careful not to jostle the packages as she made her way towards the bed. However, she failed to notice a feather duster lying, half concealed, under the bed and tripped forward, spilling the packages onto the bed.

5 Mischief in the House

"I'm so sorry" Lily exclaimed, as she reached to gather up the tumbled packages.

Daisy quickly rushed over to Lily's side, her eyes filled with concern. "Don't worry about the packages, Lily. Are you alright?"

Lily blushed, feeling a little embarrassed but unharmed. "I'm fine. Just a little slip, that's all."

Bending down to retrieve the feather duster, Daisy let out a knowing sigh. "I have a feeling I know who's responsible for this," she remarked, eyeing the mislaid duster, "Zip."

"Zip?" Lily asked, confused.

Before Lily could utter another word, Daisy called out for Zip, his name echoing down the hall like a melodious summons. In a flurry of excitement, the fluffy cloud of white fur known as Zip bounded into the room. Zip was Mrs. Winchester's beloved terrier, a charming little creature with a mischievous twinkle in his dark eyes. He was small in size but big in personality, his wagging tail and bouncy demeanor captivating anyone who crossed his path.

Daisy held the retrieved feather duster in her hands, and Zip couldn't contain his excitement, prancing around her feet, his eyes fixated on the object of his fascination. The feather duster, with its delicate plumes, had found its way into Zip's possession through one of his well-known escapades.

Earlier that morning, as one of the hardworking maids went about her cleaning duties, Zip had spotted the feather duster, perched innocently against a wall. Unable to resist the allure of the fluffy feathers, he had seized the opportunity to play and whisked it away, evading the maid's attention.

Now as Lily and Daisy exchanged amused glances, a figure approached the doorway. It was Mrs. Jenkins, a tidy middle-aged woman in a smart uniform, who had been drawn by the noise. With a knowing smile, the head housekeeper surveyed the scene, her hands resting confidently on her hips. Playfully adopting a mock expression of anger, she scolded Zip, the mischievous culprit.

"Well, well, there you are!" Mrs. Jenkins exclaimed, her tone infused with good-natured exasperation. "Zip, you are quite the mischief-maker, aren't you? When one of the upstairs maids reported a missing feather duster, I felt certain I knew who was responsible."

Zip, the playful pup, wagged his tail and let out a series of joyful barks, as if acknowledging his prank. Mrs. Jenkins, with a chuckle, tenderly patted him on the head before retrieving the feather duster from Miss Daisy.

Her gaze then shifted to Lily, curiosity evident in her eyes. "And who do we have here?" she asked, smiling warmly.

"Mrs. Jenkins, allow me to introduce you to Lily Rivera. She's our dear neighbor from a few farms over and attends school with Mr. Hansen's boys," Daisy explained.

Mrs. Jenkins extended her hand, eyes brimming with warmth, "It is a pleasure to make your acquaintance, Lily," she declared.

With manners her mother would have been proud of, Lily replied, taking Mrs. Jenkins' hand in her own. "Thank you, ma'am, it's a pleasure to meet you too," she said sincerely.

Then with introductions completed, Mrs. Jenkins bid them farewell, the feather duster in hand, and Zip excitedly bounding behind her.

"Well, Lily," said Daisy, as she finished resettling the packages on her bed, "I shall walk you back to the yard or I'm afraid you may not find your way. Even walking the halls every day, I sometimes wonder what I'll find when I turn a corner!"

Lily followed Daisy out of her room, down the polished hallway, and down several flights of stairs. She couldn't say for sure, but it seemed like the rooms they passed going down weren't even the same ones they had passed on their way up.

6 Mysterious Happenings

When Lily approached the Winchester House a few days later, a sense of unease settled over her. The usually bustling work yard was now shrouded in silence. Whispers hung in the air, carrying rumors of mysterious happenings. She noticed Carl and Theodore huddled together near the barn, their brows furrowed with worry.

"What's the matter?" Lily asked, her voice filled with concern.

Carl looked up, his eyes wide. "Lily, you won't believe what we heard. Mrs. Winchester's necklace, the one her late husband gave her, has been stolen."

Lily gasped, her mind racing with questions. "Stolen? But who would do such a thing? And why?"

Carl shook his head, his voice tinged with disbelief. "We don't know, Lily. We've been thinking about it all morning, and it just doesn't make sense. None of the workers would do something like that. They've been here for years, and they respect Mrs. Winchester. No one would want to make her sad like that."

Theodore nodded and then dropping his voice he added, "Some folks are saying it must've been a ghost. And I think they might be right."

"A ghost?" Lily asked, surprised. She could hardly believe grown-ups would think ghosts were real. "That can't be true, can it?"

Carl nodded, his expression serious. "People are saying that the necklace holds powers, that it's tied to the spirits Mrs. Winchester tries to communicate with."

Now Lily understood the quiet of the work yard. If people thought the necklace had some special powers or that ghosts were involved, they wouldn't be able to think about much else. And when it came to a place like the Winchester House, there were plenty of rumors and legends to keep ideas of unexplained mystery going. Some folks insisted the house was haunted. They claimed to have heard whispering voices and glimpsed spirits gliding through its halls. Others said the house contained secret passageways and hidden rooms to allow escape from angry phantoms.

Poor Mrs. Winchester, missing the necklace that reminded her of happier days, and now with everyone thinking her house was haunted.

"We need to uncover the truth," Lily exclaimed.

The boys exchanged determined glances, their curiosity fueling their determination. "But Lily," Theodore reminded her, "we're not supposed to be in the house."

Lily nodded, her eyes gleaming with purpose. "I know, but if we're quiet and careful, we can gather clues without anyone knowing. We'll find the truth, and maybe even the stolen necklace! First, we need a map."

Lily crouched down and began sketching the floor plan of the Winchester House in the dirt with a sharp stick, her memory capturing the path she had taken while following Miss Daisy with the packages. Carl and Theodore eagerly contributed additional details they had gleaned from their father or glimpsed through windows and doorways.

"I remember father telling us about the staircase with the spiderweb stained glass window," said Carl, adding the stairs to the growing map.

Theodore chimed in, beginning to trace out a square, "And this is where I saw the organ through the window. Some days they leave the window open and you can hear the music."

Their excitement grew with every new room they added to their map of the house. Together, they formed a plan to investigate the house's secrets, hoping to unveil the truth behind the theft and the spectral presence that loomed over the Winchester House.

7 Shadows of the Unknown

Under the cloak of darkness, Lily, Carl, and Theodore gathered near the Winchester House, their hearts pounding with a mix of eagerness and fear. It was well past sunset, and the moon cast an eerie glow upon the sprawling mansion's intricate architecture.

"Are you both ready?" Lily whispered, her voice barely audible amidst the stillness of the night.

Carl and Theodore nodded, their eyes gleaming with excitement and nervous energy. "We're ready," Carl replied, his voice filled with determination.

The trio approached the back of the house where a kitchen window was the designated entry point to their daring exploration. The kitchen staff had long departed for the night, leaving the room empty and silent. Carl climbed up onto a woodbox under the window and with a careful tug, managed to shift it open, creating a narrow passage into the mysterious world beyond.

As they slipped inside, their senses heightened, acutely aware of their surroundings. Shadows danced upon the walls as moonlight filtered through the ornate windows, casting peculiar shapes upon the floor. The sound of hammers and tools echoed from distant corners of the house, a reminder that work on the mansion persisted even through the night.

The kitchen's angles and dark corners seemed as if they might conceal mysterious figures, while the sharp knives, left out to dry on a cotton towel atop the counter, gleamed ominously. The many doors held the potential for a monstrous surprise that might burst forth at any moment. The children stood frozen, their hearts pounding, until Lily broke the silence with a deep breath, reassuring herself as much as Carl and Theodore. "It's just a kitchen, a simple, ordinary kitchen," she uttered.

"That's right," Carl chimed in, summoning the courage he might not have entirely felt but aimed to display for his younger brother.

Theodore looked from Carl to Lily and then visibly relaxed. "Alright then, let's go," he declared.

The children ventured deeper into the house, guided only by their curiosity and a sliver of moonlight illuminating their path. With every step, they marveled at the peculiarities of the house. They opened doors only to find blank walls. They peered through windows that offered glimpses of other rooms rather than the view outside. They encountered stairs with short risers, so that each step they took felt like they were falling forward, and a ceiling so low that only Theodore walked comfortably upright. At the top of the stairs they stopped, uncertain of which way to proceed.

"Which way should we go now?" Theodore whispered, squinting his eyes in the dim light.

They all tried to recall the makeshift map they had sketched in the dirt of the work yard, but they knew that at this point they were completely turned around. And they were no closer to knowing what might have happened to Mrs. Winchester's missing necklace.

"Let's try this way," Carl suggested, pointing towards the hallway to the left, its walls adorned with shadowy doorways and wallpaper patterns resembling eerie faces peering out at them. "Or maybe that way," he changed his mind and indicated the opposite direction where the dark hallway ended in a stained glass window intricately designed to look like a spider's web.

In the end, they opted for the left and cautiously made their way down the hall, peering into the shadows and listening keenly for any sounds.

As they continued their exploration, the children couldn't help but speculate quietly about the mysterious things they had seen. Wondering about the bizarre doors leading to nowhere, Theodore pondered aloud, "Why would anyone build a door that doesn't go anywhere?"

Carl, his voice filled with sympathy, replied, "Maybe Mrs. Winchester had a reason. She's known to believe in spirits and unusual things. Perhaps these doors were meant to connect her to the spirit world."

Just as the words left Carl's lips, a faint sound reached their ears — a murmuring voice, tinged with an air of mystery. It seemed to be coming from a nearby room. The mysterious chants and eerie vibrations sent shivers down their spines, reminding them of the otherworldly forces rumored to inhabit the house. The children exchanged glances, their eyes widening in surprise.

"Is that... Mrs. Winchester?" Lily asked, her voice barely above a whisper.

Carl nodded solemnly, his eyes reflecting a mix of fascination and fear. "It sounds like it," he affirmed. "They say she holds séances, you know, gatherings where people try to communicate with spirits."

Theodore's sympathetic tone returned. "Poor Mrs. Winchester. She must miss her family so much."

As they ventured further, their senses heightened. Strange noises echoed through the halls, their origins shrouded in mystery. Were they echoes of the ongoing construction or something more supernatural? The air crackled with an inexplicable energy, leaving the children unsure of what was real and what was imagined.

Their nerves frayed, the trio suddenly found themselves disoriented. The maze-like passages entwined around them like a perplexing puzzle, obscuring any sense of direction. Panic gripped them as they realized they were lost within the vast expanse of the house.

A rustle of movement behind them caused them to whirl around, their eyes scanning the dimly lit hallway. Shadows danced and flickered, playing tricks on their minds. Every creak and groan magnified in their ears, amplifying their fears.

Desperate to escape the maze of halls, they stumbled upon a passage currently under construction. With a glimmer of hope, they pushed open the heavy door at the end, only to be greeted by an eerie sight. Instead of finding a continuation of the house, they found themselves staring into the depths of the unknown — a void of darkness that seemed to stretch infinitely.

8 A Chance Encounter

"Lily? Carl? Theodore?" Daisy's voice was filled with relief as she caught up to the children in the dimly lit hallway. "Come away from there," Daisy called, waving the children away from the open door which led to nothing other than a terrifying fall to the yard below. The children, overcome with a mix of surprise and relief, breathed a collective sigh.

"Miss Daisy!" Theodore exclaimed, rushing forward away from the terrifying drop, "We're so glad it's you and not a ghost!"

Daisy laughed softly, her eyes sparkling in the dim light. "No ghosts here, I assure you. What in the world are you all doing here and so late at night?"

Carl, his voice tinged with urgency, explained the situation. "We heard about Mrs. Winchester's missing necklace."

Lily chimed in, "People are saying it might have been taken by a ghost, and we wanted to help."

Daisy's expression softened, understanding the children's concern. "I appreciate your bravery, but it's awfully late for you to be sneaking around the house. Let's find a safer place to talk," she said, guiding the children away from the hallway with its incomplete construction and the doorway with its perilous drop.

The group found a nearby alcove, tucked away from prying eyes and wandering spirits. Inside, two small velvet couches faced each other, separated by a delicately carved table. It was a cozy spot amidst the vastness of the mansion. Daisy gracefully settled onto one of the couches, her gaze meeting the children's with a blend of curiosity and concern.

"So, you've heard about the missing necklace," she began, her voice tinged with worry. "Poor Aunt Sallie has been so distraught about it. But as for ghosts? I'm not so sure about that."

Theodore leaned forward, his voice laced with interest. "Do you have any ideas about what might have happened?"

Daisy nodded, her mind delving into possibilities. "Well, on the day the necklace went missing, there were extra workers in the house. They were hanging new wallpaper in the east wing. It's usually the same familiar faces around here, but the new special wallpaper I showed you the other day needed particular care in the hanging."

The children exchanged glances, their minds racing with the newfound information. The mention of the workers sparked their curiosity and provided a potential lead in their search for the truth.

"So, it could have been one of those workers who took the necklace?" Lily suggested, her voice filled with determination.

Daisy nodded in agreement. "Yes, that's certainly a possibility. However, I think it's best for us to leave the investigation to the officials. In two days' time, Aunt Sallie's attorney will arrive to file the insurance claim for the necklace, and with any luck, all this talk of ghosts will fade away."

Her gaze shifted from Lily to Carl, and finally to Theodore, whose drowsy head was beginning to rest on the cushions of the small couch. "And now, it's time for you children to be headed home to bed before your own parents start worrying that ghosts have spirited you away too." She leaned over, gently taking Theodore's hand, and rose to guide the children out of the house.

Confidently leading the way, Miss Daisy guided the children through the hallways and down the stairs, which appeared much less foreboding in her cheerful company. When they reached the back door she gave them a reassuring wave and bid them goodbye. As they exchanged farewells, the children's minds buzzed with thoughts of the missing necklace and the workers who could hold the key to unraveling the mystery.

9 Unanswered Questions

The morning sun bathed the Winchester farm in a warm glow as Lily arrived to find Carl and Theodore eagerly waiting for her near the barn. Their faces were brimming with excitement, and Lily could hardly contain her curiosity.

"We have some news, Lily!" Carl exclaimed, his eyes shining with anticipation. "I was asking our dad about the men who came to hang the wallpaper. Who they were, where they were from.

He told me he thought they were from the city but that if I wanted to know I should ask Frank."

Theodore nodded in agreement, his voice excited, "Dad said Frank helped with the wallpaper hanging. Apparently, one of their workers fell ill, so they needed an extra pair of hands."

Lily's eyebrows furrowed as she absorbed the information. "That's curious. Maybe Frank can tell us more about what happened."

The trio made their way to the bustling yard, their eyes scanning the busy scene until they spotted Frank. Frank stood tall among the crew, his dark hair framing his face and an ever-present friendly smile. Excitement filled the children as they approached him, eager to gather any piece of information that could bring them closer to solving the mystery.

"Hi, Frank!" Carl greeted him with a cheerful grin. "We heard you helped the wallpaper crew the other day. Can you tell us anything about them?"

Frank leaned against a stack of wooden boards, wiping his hands on a rag. "Sure thing," he replied, his voice tinged with curiosity. "Those guys seemed nice, for the most part. But this one fella, George, didn't sit right with me. I told your father that if they bring the crew back for any more wallpapering, they might want to tell them to leave that fella behind."

The children's eyes widened with interest, hanging on Frank's every word.

"You see George kept asking these questions about the house and Mrs. Winchester and he kept poking his nose into places he shouldn't be," Frank continued, his brow furrowing with disapproval. "Once when we were all supposed to be working, I heard Zip barking up a storm, and when I went to see what was going on, I caught George lurking outside one of Mrs. Winchester's bedrooms. He tried to excuse himself, claiming he had simply lost his way, but truth be told, he had no business wandering around where he didn't belong in the first place."

"One of Mrs. Winchester's bedrooms?" Theodore asked, confused.

"Well, Theodore," Frank said, lowering his voice, "Mrs. Winchester never sleeps in the same bedroom two nights in a row. Do you know why?" he asked, leaning closer to Theodore.

"No, why?" asked Theodore, his eyes wide.

"The ghosts!" Frank exclaimed, jumping at Theodore. For a moment, Theodore looked scared, then Frank started to laugh, and Theodore, Carl, and Lily all joined in. "Really though, it beats me, Theodore," Frank shrugged and stood up, "I've only got one bedroom, but Mrs. Winchester, she's got more than 30 of them, so maybe she just wants to try them all out."

Lily's mind raced with possibilities. "Did you see him anywhere else, Frank?"

Frank nodded, his expression turning serious as a frown appeared on his face. "You know, at the end of the day, I spotted him wandering around the yard and over near the barn. Seemed like he was up to no good, if you ask me."

The children exchanged glances, their suspicions growing stronger by the minute. The mysterious man's behavior seemed far from innocent, and they couldn't shake the feeling that he might be connected to the missing necklace.

"Do you think George could've taken Mrs. Winchester's necklace?" Lily asked, looking from Frank to Carl and Theodore.

"As soon as I heard that Mrs. Winchester's necklace was missing, I thought of George, standing outside of her bedroom door. I told your father," Frank said, glancing between Carl and Theodore, "and he let the police know, but when they questioned George and even searched his rooms, they came up empty-handed."

With that news, the children's excited expressions changed to looks of puzzlement.

"Thank you, Frank," said Carl and with a final nod, Frank bid them farewell, returning to his work.

The children walked back through the work yard scuffing the toes of their shoes in the dry dirt.

Theodore was the first to speak, "I thought for sure it would be that George. What else was he doing outside Mrs. Winchester's room if not stealing the necklace?"

"I thought so too," said Carl, "but the police searched him, and he didn't have it. Looks like that lead turned out to be a dead end."

"Maybe it was ghosts after all," said Theodore with a hopeless shrug.

10 The Mysteries Multiply

Lily, Carl, and Theodore walked across the Winchester work yard, their minds still abuzz with the mystery surrounding Mrs. Winchester's missing necklace. As they approached the barn, their attention was caught by a distressed moaning sound coming from within. They exchanged worried glances before rushing inside.

Inside the barn, they found Lulubelle, the newly arrived cow, pacing anxiously. Her previously calm demeanor was replaced by restlessness, and her eyes were filled with unease.

"Oh no, what's wrong with Lulubelle?" Lily exclaimed, concern etched on her face.

Carl approached the cow cautiously, his voice soothing. "Easy, girl. It's okay. We're here to help."

Theodore joined in, trying to calm Lulubelle with gentle strokes along her back. "Something must have spooked her. But what could it be?"

As they pondered the cause of Lulubelle's distress, their attention was diverted by the sight of a maid, bustling about near an outdoor shed. It was Katie, a hardworking young woman Carl and Theodore knew well. She was struggling to carry a large wash tub, her expression a mix of annoyance and bewilderment.

Feeling curious about the commotion, Theodore approached Katie, his voice laced with wonder. "Excuse me, Katie, but what are you doing with that wash tub?"

The young woman paused, wiping a bead of sweat from her brow. "Oh, dear," she sighed. "Mrs. Jenkins told me that Zip needs a thorough wash. He showed up at the house covered in hay and dirt."

Understanding dawned on Lily's face as she connected the dots. "Maybe it was Zip who upset Lulubelle."

A weary smile crossed Katie's lips. "That may be. Zip left a trail of hay right through the ballroom and into the sitting room. Mrs. Jenkins is quite upset. It'll take a lot of effort to clean it all up."

"We could bathe Zip!" Theodore exclaimed. He loved the spunky white pup and took any chance he got to play with him.

"Sure," said Carl, a grin spreading across his face, "we'll make sure he's squeaky clean."

"That would be an enormous help," said Katie, as Lily and Carl reached to take the wash tub from her. Carrying the tub to the rear of the laundry room, the children positioned it near a back door.

Katie entered the house and soon emerged from the door carrying the wriggling, hay-covered Zip. The pup's fur was tangled and dirty, showing evidence of his recent adventure in the barn. The smell of manure clung to him, a lingering reminder of his mischief. Despite his messy look, Zip's eyes sparkled with excitement, as if he was proud of his exploration.

"Thank you, children," Katie said gratefully, lowering Zip into Theodore's waiting arms, "this will be a big help. I still can't believe that this little rascal made it through the ballroom, parlor, and right into the sitting room in this state."

"Sounds like he was intent on getting where he wanted to go," said Lily, rubbing the little dog's cheerful face.

Lily was just beginning to wonder where the children would get the water to fill the wash tub when Katie, who had returned inside, once again emerged. This time she was carrying a length of coiled up tubing and had a basket of towels and a bar of soap hanging over her arm. Carl positioned the end of the tube in the tub, and in a moment, water poured forth into the waiting tub.

Lily's eyes widened in astonishment. While she had heard that Mrs. Winchester's home had the luxury of indoor running water, a rarity among the neighboring farms, including her own, she had never imagined a hose for water coming right out of the house.

Katie bid the children farewell with an appreciative smile, then retreated into the house to tackle the task of sweeping up the scattered hay.

Once the tub was filled, and the water turned off, Theodore gently lowered Zip into the tub. Carl worked the bar of soap into a lather over the little dog's fur, while Lily and Theodore fawned over him, telling him what a good boy he was.

Once the bath was complete, the children reached for towels and lovingly dried Zip's fluffy, white fur. The little dog responded with joyful barks, playfully dancing on his hind legs. He reveled in the attention lavished upon him, his tail wagging with enthusiasm.

Katie reappeared to retrieve the now clean and exuberant pup, while Carl and Lily efficiently emptied the tub. Once the task was done, the children found themselves once again pondering the ongoing mysteries.

"It just doesn't make sense to me," said Carl, "Why would Zip have been in Lulubelle's stall? He almost never leaves the house and garden. What could have enticed him out here to the work yard?" he wondered.

"The missing necklace, that strange fella from the wallpaper crew, Lulubelle upset, and Zip in the barn," pondered Theodore aloud, "I for one don't think it's ghosts, but there sure do seem to be a lot of strange things happening at Winchester Ranch lately."

"You're right, Theodore," said Lily, "too many strange things to be a coincidence. I have an idea, but it's going to mean another late night. Are you up for it?" she asked her friends.

11 A Suspect in the Barn

As the sun dipped below the horizon, casting long shadows across the Winchester barnyard, Lily, Carl, and Theodore gathered at their designated meeting spot. A sense of anticipation filled the air, and the weight of their mission settled on their shoulders. They planned to stake out the barn, hoping to catch any suspicious activity under the cover of dusk.

As the hours passed, the darkness intensified. The moon's pale light cast twisted shadows across the scene. Machinery sat silently like skeletal frames. The glint of moonlight on stacked tools gave them an unsettling gleam. The tractors, with their hulking forms, seemed to offer hiding places for so many sinister possibilities.

Lily scanned their surroundings, her voice tinged with a touch of unease. "Let's stay calm, but stay alert. We need to be observant, and we might just find the answers we're looking for."

Carl nodded, his gaze nervously sweeping the area around the barnyard. "You're right. We can't miss a thing. This might be our chance to uncover the truth."

Time passed slowly, and doubt began to gnaw at their resolve. The night seemed too quiet, devoid of any signs of trouble. But just as their hope wavered, a figure emerged from the shadows, creeping along the edge of the yard toward the barn.

Intrigued and cautious, the children silently moved closer, their eyes fixed on the mysterious man. He slipped into Lulubelle's stall, digging frantically in a corner of the hay. It was evident he expected to find something there, but his frustration grew as his search left him empty-handed.

Lulubelle, with her delicate temperament, was clearly distressed by this stranger digging around in her stall. Her gentle moos were filled with unease. The children exchanged worried glances, unsure of how to intervene.

Carl whispered, "Let's make some noise and scare him off."

Lilly nodded in agreement and pointed at a nearby collection of farm tools. Carl followed her, and they quietly made their selections from the shovels, hand rakes, and pitchforks. With trembling hands, they banged the tools together, creating a clamor that pierced the evening air. Theodore joined in, cupping his hands around his mouth and emitting an eerie sound that brought to mind spooks and specters.

Startled by the strange commotion, the man froze, his eyes darting around in alarm. Whether he suspected the noise was caused by one of the groups of nighttime laborers returning to the work yard or by one of the fabled ghosts from the legends surrounding the Winchester Ranch, he abandoned his search and fled into the darkness.

Relieved and excited, the children cautiously entered the barn. Lulubelle, grateful for their presence, nuzzled against them. Theodore reached into his pocket and produced a carrot, offering it to the cow who eagerly accepted the treat.

As they fed Lulubelle, the realization dawned upon them. The man who had stolen the necklace had hidden it in the stall, intending to retrieve it later. But if the man didn't find the necklace, where could it be? It was then that Lily and Carl exchanged a knowing glance, a shared understanding passing between them.

Theodore, puzzled, asked, "What's going on? Where is the necklace?"

Lily couldn't help but smile. "The man who was here digging in Lulubelle's stall was George, from the wallpapering crew. He had stolen the necklace and hidden it here in Lulubelle's stall to collect later. But while we were trying to recover Mrs. Winchester's necklace, someone else was too, someone who cares about her very deeply."

Carl chimed in, his voice filled with amusement. "Zip is the one who took the necklace from the barn. But he wasn't stealing it. He was trying to return the necklace, just like we are."

The realization sparked a renewed sense of purpose in the children. They now knew that the necklace was close, within their reach. With Zip as their unlikely ally, they were determined to return the precious heirloom to its rightful owner and bring an end to the mystery of the missing necklace.

12 Following the Trail

Excitement buzzed in the air as Lily, Carl, and Theodore hurried into the Winchester barnyard early the next morning, their steps brimming with anticipation as they sought out Miss Daisy. Upon seeing their eager faces, Miss Daisy couldn't help but smile. Before she could even utter a word, the children burst out in a flurry of overlapping voices, each vying to tell the tale. Daisy raised a hand, her gentle voice calling for calm. "Hold on, hold on, one at a time! Take a breath and tell me what happened."

They took a collective breath and began recounting the events of the previous night. Their words spilled out, describing the stakeout at the barn, the mysterious man's intrusion, and Lulubelle's distress. Daisy's eyes widened in amazement and concern as she listened intently to their tale.

"You were in real danger," Daisy exclaimed, her voice filled with genuine worry. "I'm relieved to see you safe."

The children reassured Daisy that they had scared the man away, their determination shining through. Lily continued, "But the man didn't find the necklace. You won't believe who has it!"

Daisy's curiosity was stirred. "Who? Who could have taken it?"

With a twinkle in their eyes, the children revealed the truth. "Zip!" they said at once.

"He must have thought it was lost and took it upon himself to find it for Mrs. Winchester," said Carl.

Daisy's astonishment mingled with delight. "Zip? Oh, that clever little dog! But where could he have hidden it?"

Lily suggested they seek out Mrs. Jenkins, the housekeeper, and inquire about the trail of hay that Zip had left throughout the house the day before. The group, led by Miss Daisy, made their way inside the magnificent Winchester House, the detailed carvings and elegant furnishings now relieved of their spooky auras in the streaming sunlight of the morning.

They followed the hum of activity, venturing into the bustling heart of the household. There they found Mrs. Jenkins presiding over the kitchen, a symphony of activity unfolding around her. The air was filled with the clattering of pots and pans, the rhythmic chopping of ingredients, and the inviting aroma of freshly brewed coffee. A team of skilled kitchen staff moved with grace and precision in their crisp white aprons. The highly polished wood countertops spoke of countless meals prepared with love and expertise. Sunlight streamed through the lace curtains, casting delicate patterns on the golden wooden floors. Mrs. Jenkins listened attentively as the children excitedly recounted the previous night's events and shared how Zip's antics had led them to believe he had hidden the necklace somewhere in the house.

"Can you show us where Zip went yesterday" asked Lily eagerly, "when he trailed the hay through the house?"

"Assuredly I can," replied Mrs. Jenkins, "I won't be forgetting that bit of mischief any time soon."

Mrs. Jenkins led the children through the grand halls of the house, each room unfolding before them in breathtaking splendor. They passed through the magnificent ballroom, where the floor boasted a mesmerizing pattern of two-tone checkerboard wood and an imposing pipe organ stood as testament to the house's grandeur. Carl elbowed Theodore, urging him to close his gaping mouth, as both boys stared, amazed at the interior of the house which they had previously only glimpsed from doorways and windows.

Continuing on, they entered a parlor with rich velvet drapes framing the windows, delicately carved chairs with needlework cushions, and portraits of intriguing figures on the walls. Lily wished she had the time to examine each of the mysterious portraits.

Finally, the group arrived at Mrs. Winchester's favorite sitting room, where Zip had ended his wild, messy run the day before. The room's walls were painted a beautiful shade of green. Peaceful paintings hung on the walls, depicting calming landscapes and scenes of relaxation. The spotless furnishings, covered in rich gold fabric, hid the fact that only the day before a scamp of a dog had tracked dirt and hay all over their seats.

"And here I found him," said Mrs. Jenkins, gesturing at a plush velvet chair, "sitting up pleased as punch, covered in hay, on the Mistress's favorite chair."

Lily's gaze fell upon the elegant chair. Acting on a hunch, she reached deep down the side of the seat cushion, her fingers brushing against something metallic and cool. With a smile, she pulled out the necklace, its delicate beauty gleaming in the morning light.

Gasps of astonishment filled the room. And then a sound from the door made them all turn as a petite frame draped in black lace entered. "Oh, my dear husband's gift. It has found its way back to me," exclaimed Mrs. Winchester softly, taking the necklace in her gloved hands.

The children all turned bashful, averting their eyes and blushing. Here was Mrs. Winchester, one of the richest women in America, owner of the mystical Winchester mansion, and herself a person of great mystery.

"It was the children who solved the mystery, Aunt Sallie," said Daisy, gesturing to Lily, Carl, and Theodore.

"Thank you so very much, children, this necklace is precious to me and without your help I might never have seen it again," said Mrs. Winchester gazing at the necklace, her face filled with sentiment.

"You're welcome, ma'am," said Lily smiling happily. She was glad they had been able to help, "but it wasn't just us ma'am. It was Zip too."

At that, Zip ran into the room and jumped onto the velvet chair. "Well," said Daisy, "in that case, I suppose everyone is in for a treat. I wonder if there's any of that delectable ice cream?" Daisy asked, the children's eyes widening at the mention of the rare, sweet treat. "And do you suppose there might be a meaty bone in the kitchen for Zip?" Daisy asked Mrs. Jenkins.

"Well," Mrs. Jenkins chimed in, with a touch of amusement in her voice, "it seems everyone is in for a delightful treat today. We have a freshly made batch of Neapolitan ice cream ready for scooping," she revealed, smiling at the children. "And I'm certain there's something for our fluffy detective as well," she said, patting the pup.

The children's faces lit up with big smiles, in anticipation of the delectable treat. They eagerly followed Mrs. Jenkins to the bright and inviting kitchen with Zip trailing along behind.

13 Sweet Reflections

As they entered the cheerful kitchen, Mrs. Jenkins turned to address Katie, the friendly young maid, who stood nearby. "Katie, can you please bring the ice cream from the icehouse for these three," she requested. "They've just solved the case of the missing necklace."

"Certainly," exclaimed Katie, her own curiosity stoked. "But then, I must hear all the exciting details." She disappeared through the back door, returning moments later, carefully cradling a ceramic crock filled with delicious Neapolitan ice cream.

Meanwhile, Mrs. Jenkins retrieved three white bowls from a cabinet. A gleaming metal scoop was selected from a drawer. And with practiced precision, she began dishing out the ice cream. Each bowl received equal portions of the delectable trio of chocolate, vanilla, and strawberry that composed the Neapolitan dessert.

Suddenly, Zip, the loyal canine, let out a soft bark, ensuring he hadn't been overlooked. Mrs. Jenkins chuckled affectionately, leaning down to present the eager pup with a meaty bone. "No one could possibly forget you, Zip."

The wag of Zip's tail radiated sheer delight, making Lily, Carl, and Theodore laugh. Mrs. Jenkins handed the children their ice cream and

Zip, carrying his bone, followed them out to the back steps.

Just as the children were starting to spoon up their delectable looking treat, Frank passed by pushing a wheelbarrow. His face lit up with excitement as he spotted them. "There you are! I've been looking for you three," he exclaimed. "You won't believe who the night crew found wandering around in the orchard last night, completely lost and ranting about ghosts or some such nonsense."

Lily, Carl, and Theodore exchanged knowing glances, and it was Theodore who spoke up confidently, "Let me guess - it was George!"

Frank's mouth fell open in surprise. "How on earth did you know that, Theodore?" Then he paused, "Or maybe it's better if you keep that a secret," he said, winking mischievously. With that, Frank continued on his way, pushing the wheelbarrow towards his next task.

The warm glow of the summer sun bathed the Winchester House, casting a golden hue upon Lily, Carl, and Theodore as they sat on the back kitchen steps, enjoying the delicious homemade ice cream. Zip happily lay at their feet working attentively at his bone. A sense of contentment settled over them, knowing that their adventure had reached a satisfying conclusion.

As they savored each spoonful, the conversation turned to the mysteries that still lingered within the grand estate. Theodore, ever the inquisitive mind, spoke up first. "You know, I heard those stairs were made short so that ghosts couldn't follow you up them."

Carl laughed and shook his head. "Ghosts don't need stairs. They float! But maybe those short steps were meant to make it harder for anyone to follow, living or otherwise."

The trio exchanged curious glances, contemplating the mysteries of the Winchester

House. They mused about the door that seemingly led to nowhere, wondering if it held a purpose beyond their understanding. Was it an entrance for spirits, or simply a construction project awaiting completion?

Lily, her eyes sparkling with excitement, spoke up. "I'm not entirely sure, but you know what? I can't wait to see what happens next in this amazing house."

The children nodded in agreement, their sense of adventure ignited by the thrill of the unknown. They had explored the depths of the Winchester House, faced their fears, and emerged with newfound courage and resilience. And though they might not have all the answers, they knew that the mystery and intrigue of this extraordinary place would continue to captivate them in ways they couldn't imagine.

As they finished their ice cream, the children shared a moment of gratitude. Grateful for their friendship, grateful for the lessons learned, and grateful for the mysteries they had experienced together.

ABOUT THE AUTHOR

Alexis Schmitz remembers her first visit to the Winchester House as a child. The intriguing history and lingering mysteries of the house stuck with her and were reignited when she took her own children for a visit years later. Alexis is a teacher with over 20 years of experience, who loves learning and teaching through creativity and exploration. She has written curriculum for elementary school, contributed to educational magazines, and is a parent to four children, whom she homeschooled for many years. Alexis loves wonderful stories - especially mysteries! She lives on the coast of central California where, in her free time, she can often be found doing her own favorite type of sleuthing - searching for sea creatures in the local tidepools.

Made in the USA
Las Vegas, NV
10 September 2023

77329225R00062